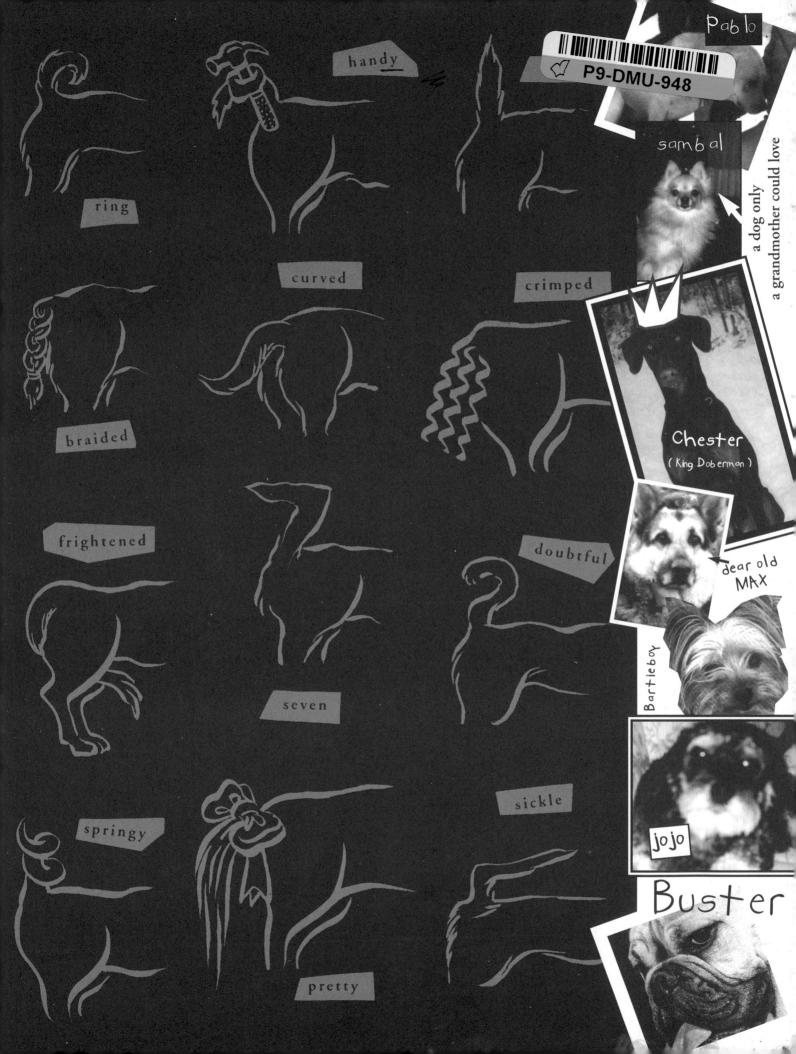

ring

handy

curved

crimped

braided

frightened

doubtful

seven

springy

sickle

pretty

Pablo

sambal

a dog only a grandmother could love

Chester
(King Doberman)

dear old MAX

Bartieboy

jojo

Buster

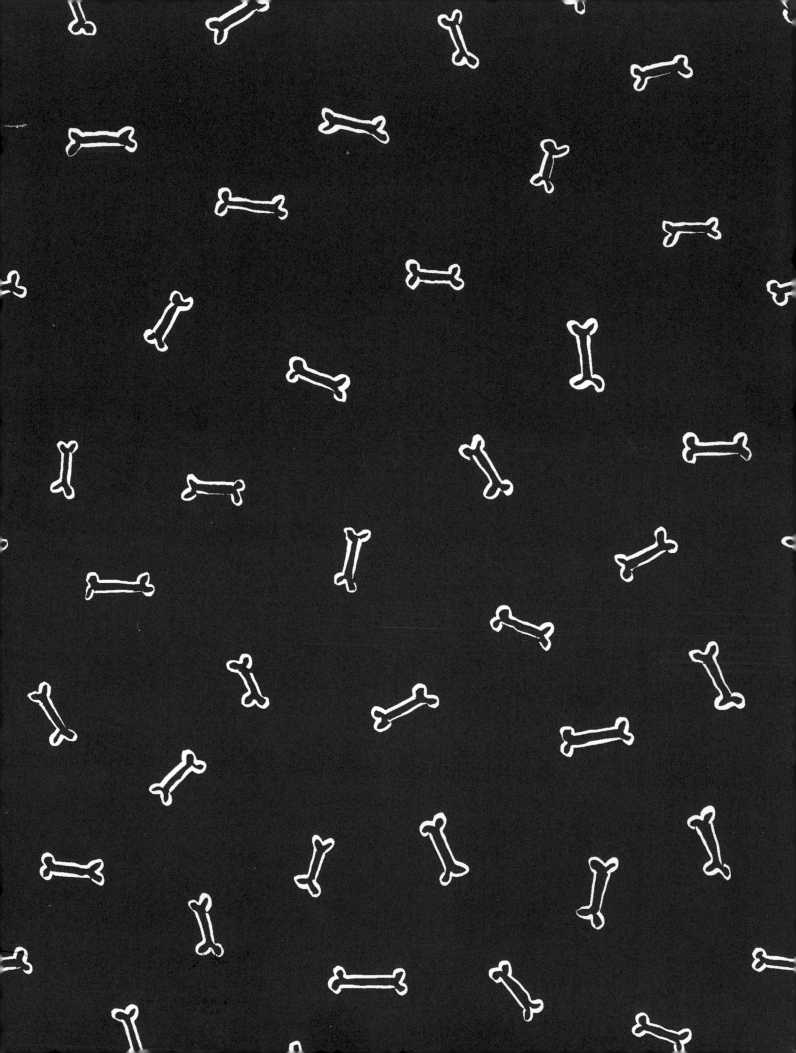

Dog Tales

Jennifer Rae

Rose Cowles

Whitecap Books
Vancouver/Toronto

Whitecap Books
Vancouver/Toronto

Edited by Allison Haupt
Cover design and interior design by Rose Cowles

Printed and bound in Canada

Canadian Cataloguing in Publication Data

Rae, Jennifer, 1966-
     Dog tales

     ISBN 1-55110-772-4

     1. Children's stories, Canadian (English)* 2. Parodies. I. Cowles, Rose, 1967- .
II. Title
PS8585.A295D63 1998   jC13'.54   C98-910659-4
PZ7.R1228Do 1998

The publisher acknowledges the support of the Canada Council for the Arts and the Cultural Services Branch of the Government of British Columbia for our publishing program. We acknowledge the financial support of the Government of Canada through the Book Industry Development Program for our publishing activities.

Pardon me, but I think there's been some kind of mistake. This is a full-color book, but we cats seem to be in black and white.

It's no mistake. I'd say it's a canine cons-purr-acy! Well, what can you expect from a book called Dog Tales?

CONTENTS

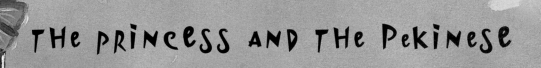

Cindersmelly

Once upon a time, there was a big black dog who loved to roll in smelly things: garbage, gym socks—even Limburger cheese if she could find it! Her name was Cindersmelly.

Cindersmelly lived with a pair of persnickety Siamese cats who spent all day grooming and cleaning themselves but who never lifted a claw around the house. Cindersmelly was made to do all the work—fetching newspapers, carrying stinky slippers, cleaning dirty dishes, even sweeping the floor with her big black tail. So not only was she smelly—she was dusty as well.

"Cindersmelly," said the cats, "you are too dusty and smelly to go to the Prince's Pet Show. Besides, you have to stay home and clean the house." So the cats preened their paws, waxed their whiskers, touched up their tails, put on their finest, fanciest collars, and off they went. Cindersmelly felt pretty down in the dumps. But the cats were right. She was rather smelly; surely too smelly to go to the show.

Suddenly, a vacuum cleaner salesman appeared at the door. "Harry Dogslobber's the name," he declared. "Might I come in?" Ordinarily, Cindersmelly didn't have

This is a good story so far.

Great story!

1

much time for salesmen, but Mr. Dogslobber's vacuum cleaner looked so bright and shiny, and she really did need help with the housework.

Slacker.

"All right," said Cindersmelly, "let's see what this thing can do." Mr. Dogslobber showed Cindersmelly all the vacuum's marvelous attachments: the Slipper-Sucker, the Paper-Picker, the Furball-Finder, the Whisker-Whisk— why, it even cleaned carpets! "And best of all," announced Mr. Dogslobber, "here is the last attachment . . . the Dog-Duster!" He produced a long coil of tubing that was silver and shiny with a special brush at one end. "Dog-Duster?" asked Cindersmelly. "Surely even a Dog-Duster couldn't dust a dog as big and smelly as me."

You said it. It's a dog's life.

No sooner had she spoken than Mr. Dogslobber attached the Dog-Duster and went to work. First, he sprinkled Cindersmelly with a whole box of baking soda. Then, he began vacuuming—right from her head to the tip of her tail! In just minutes, the job was done. There was Cindersmelly, as big as ever, but clean and shiny—and no longer smelly!

"I could almost go to the pet show like this," announced Cindersmelly. "Except that I have no collar special enough and no way to get there." Well, Harry Dogslobber had a soft spot for dogs. He'd had a dog himself when he was a boy. "Look," he said, "you can take the vacuum. It's pretty powerful—I drove it here myself.

And now . . . we will make you a collar!" And with that, he slipped the coiled, silver Dog-Duster around Cindersmelly's neck. It was a perfect fit! "Off you go," said Harry Dogslobber. "But please . . . bring the vacuum back in one hour! I have other calls to make today."

Off went Cindersmelly to the Prince's Pet Show. Mr. Dogslobber was right—the vacuum was fast and Cindersmelly was there in no time flat. As soon as she entered the pet show a hush fell. Truly, Cindersmelly was the biggest, blackest animal there by far. "What a magnificent creature!" the Prince exclaimed. "What a beautiful shiny black coat! I should like to have such a big, black dog as that!" Cindersmelly was flattered. Surely a prince's dog wouldn't have to spend all day doing housework.

Before Cindersmelly knew it, the hour was up and she had to get the vacuum back to Harry Dogslobber. So with her head held low and her tail between her legs, Cindersmelly slipped out a side door. As she did so, her elegant, coiled collar—the silver Dog-Duster— became caught and was pulled from her neck. But Cindersmelly was too dejected to even notice. Up she hopped onto the vacuum cleaner and sped home.

The next day, Cindersmelly was cleaning the house while the lazy Siamese cats lay about snoozing and scratching the furniture, when another caller appeared at the door. This time it was not a salesman, it was the Prince himself . . . holding the silver Dog-Duster!

"I am searching for the animal who wore this elegant collar to the pet show yesterday," he announced. The cats seized the Duster between them. "Let me try it on!" they both squealed. "Surely it is one of our collars." But the collar was too big. Even for the two of them together.

"Doesn't anyone else live here?" asked the Prince. "Surely it is not Cindersmelly's!" the cats whined. "She is just a smelly old dog!" But sure enough, when Cindersmelly slipped the Dog-Duster on, it fit perfectly! The Prince was thrilled. "I hereby appoint you Your Royal Houndness!" he declared.

Cindersmelly turned to the wretched Siamese cats. "The next time a fellow named Harry Dogslobber comes calling," she said, "you had better invite him in. You will be needing a vacuum cleaner!" And off went Cindersmelly with the Prince. 🦴

What kind of a Prince chooses a big stinky dog over two elegant cats?

This story certainly had a miserable ending! I thought fairy tales were supposed to have happy endings!

This isn't a fairy tale— it's a dog tale!

LittLe ReD RiDiNG HouND

Once upon a time, there lived a lovely little hound with a beautiful, silky red coat. One day she was sniffing and snuffling her way through the dark woods when she ran into an evil cat.

Wait a minute. An evil cat? Why does the cat have to be evil?

Why can't the dog be evil? Evil Red Riding Hound, that should be the name of this story!

"Where are you going?" asked the cat. Ordinarily the little hound didn't speak to strangers. "Always keep your nose to the ground!" her mother had told her. But it was only a cat. "Why, I'm going to my granny's house to give her these biscuits," replied the hound. "Biscuits, eh?" asked the cat. "Hmmmm. I'll tell you a short-cut to your granny's house." So he did, and off snuffled the hound in another direction.

"Purrrrr-fect," snickered the evil cat. "Now I shall get to Granny's house first. That dog's pretty dumb—I bet if I dressed up as old

Granny, she'd give *me* those biscuits." So off the evil cat raced through the dark woods.

When the cat got to Granny's house, Little Red Riding Hound was already there! The cat was purr-plexed. "How did you get here so quickly?" he asked. "Well, I did get lost at first," she replied, "but not for long! I am a hound after all, so I just sniffed and snuffled and followed my nose till I found my way. I found an even better short-cut than the one you told me about!" And with that, the hound shut the door.

"Hot dog!" exclaimed Granny. "What a great nose you have!" And they sat down for biscuits, while the cat outside had none.

The cat gets nothing? I don't like this story.

Don't worry. They were probably dog biscuits anyway.

10

JACK RUSSELL
AND THE BEANSTALK

Oh, come on now. Dogs can't climb trees. That's dogsense.

Cat-agorically impossible! Climbing is cat business!

Once upon a time, in a merry old place called England, there lived an earnest little dog named Jack Russell. Jack had lots of good qualities—he was quick, he could crawl into small spaces, he could even climb trees. But Jack did have a few short-comings. For one thing, he was determined. Doggedly determined. And he was stubborn. In fact, Jack was downright dogmatic.

One day a sly stray dog approached Jack as he was guarding his family's enormous bone collection. The stray dog took one look at Jack's big pile of bones and said, "There's just no way I could possibly trade my three magic beans, even for all those bones." "Magic beans?" asked Jack quizzically. "What is so special about three beans that you would not trade them for this fine collection of bones?" But the stray was clever. "I mustn't tell you," he said. "If I did, you would certainly want them. You would beg me to trade my magic beans for your bones." Well, that was it. Jack was determined. He wanted those beans! Being a proud little dog Jack was normally above begging, but he simply had to

11

have those beans. So Jack begged. He begged and begged. And sure enough, Jack got the three magic beans and away went the stray dog with all of Jack's bones!

When Jack's mother discovered what he had done, she wasn't too pleased. "Jack," she said, "for a clever little dog, that wasn't very smart. Three beans isn't even enough for dinner. Besides, we're dogs, not vegetarians!" "But Mom," exclaimed Jack, "these aren't just *any* old beans. They're *magic* beans!"

But to tell you the truth, even Jack was beginning to have doubts. Now that he looked at the beans, they didn't look that special. They actually looked like rather ordinary beans. But Jack was stubborn. And he was determined. So he went out to the garden, diligently dug three little holes, and planted the beans.

When Jack awoke the next morning and looked out his window,

he saw an amazing thing. An immense beanstalk stretched far into the sky! Even Jack's mother was impressed. "You see," Jack said. "I *told* you they were magic beans." "Well then," said Jack's mother, "you'd better climb up that beanstalk and take a look around. See if you can find the burglar who took our bones." So Jack went up, up, up the beanstalk. When he got to the top, Jack looked all around. He couldn't see any bones. He couldn't see the sly stray dog. What he saw instead was a huge castle.

Jack was dumbfounded but he was also determined. Jack trotted over and squeezed under the castle door.

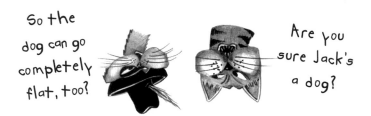

So the dog can go completely flat, too?

Are you sure Jack's a dog?

Inside, Jack came face-to-face with a big Bloodhound. "Wow!" said Jack. "You are huge!"

Boy, Jack really knows how to flatter a lady!

"I am pretty big," said the Bloodhound, "but you should see my husband. He's a Great Dane! Here he comes now!" Jack heard the Great Dane's thundering pawsteps, loud ear-flappings, wet snufflings and grumbling grunts, and decided not to stick around. He hopped up into the oven and hid.

In came the giant drooling Great Dane, carrying a big bag of bones that he had likely stolen. "Flea, fly, toad, frog," boomed the Great Dane, "I smell the fur of an English-dog! Be he a Lab or be he a Poodle, I'll squeeze him into a canine strudel!" "Stop being so dramatic," said his wife. "Sit yourself down and have a catnap. You're always cranky before your nap."

The Great Dane set down his bag of bones, turned around six times and fell fast asleep. And quick as a rabbit, Jack leaped from the oven and grabbed the bag of bones. Off he went, past the Bloodhound, out the window and down the beanstalk as fast as his little legs could carry him!

Jack arrived back home dog-tired but triumphant. "Did you get back our bones?" asked his mother. "No, I didn't," said Jack. "But I found an even BIGGER bone collection and these bones are worth far more than three magic beans!" Jack's mother was amazed. "You *are* a bright little dog, Jack," she said. And you know what? She was right.

What? Jack steals a bag of bones and everyone thinks he's smart?

That's dogsense for you.

15

THe PRINCESS AND THe PeKINESe

Once upon a time, there lived a petulant little Prince. The Prince had everything he could want. He had a pony and a purple parrot. He had a pushed-in Pug dog and a pompadoured Poodle. He had a polka-dotted Pit Bull. He even had a prized Pekinese. But the precocious Prince cared little for his pets. What he wanted most of all was a Princess.

He didn't have everything.

What about a cat? He didn't have a cat?

One evening in the midst of a terrible storm, a bedraggled, soaked-through Princess came to the door. At least, she said she was a Princess. But the Prince was skeptical. "How do I know you're a real Princess?" asked the Prince. "Because I told you I am," replied the Princess. Still, the Prince was not convinced.

That night, before bedtime, the peevish little Prince snuck into the guest room. First, he tucked his pushed-in Pug dog under the mattress. But he was too small. Then, he stuffed in his pompadoured Poodle. But he was too soft. He even tried the polka-dotted Pit Bull. But he was too hard. Finally, he squeezed his prized Pekinese under the mattress. Perfect! Then he took nineteen more mattresses and piled them on top.

What about the dog?

Relat. It's only a dog!

"That's a pretty big bed!" thought the Princess. But she was tired, so she just climbed on top. Yet try as she might, the Princess slept hardly a wink all night. "What a rotten bed!" she said the next morning. The Prince realized at once that she must be a real Princess to have felt such a small Pekinese through twenty mattresses. No one but a real Princess could do that! Even the dog was impressed (though a bit wrinkled).

But when the Princess found out what the Prince had done, she was positively persnickety. "I told you I was a real Princess, but you didn't believe me. And you're mean, too. Only a nasty person would stuff his dog under twenty mattresses!" So she picked up the Pekinese, tucked him under her arm and took him home to her castle, where they lived happily ever after. 🦴

Rapawnzul

Rapawnzul was a spaniel
with long, majestic ears.
She'd lived within the castle walls
for many happy years.

Her ears were oh-so-heavy,
they both swung to-and-fro.
She piled them high upon her head
and tied them in a bow.

She loved to chase the castle squirrels
around the castle trees.
She loved to chase the wicked witch's
evil Siamese.

She loved to roam the castle garden
howling at the moon.
And all the kingdom marveled
at her sweet and soulful tune.

One day the witch's wretched cat
dared to venture near.
He saw Rapawnzul sleeping
and he whispered in her ear.

"I place upon you silly dog,
an evil Siamese curse.
That only can be broken if
you're spoken to in verse.

"Your ears will always trip you up,
they'll always come unbound.
And you will be imprisoned
so you can't chase me around!"

When poor Rapawnzul woke up
she was utterly alone.
And locked within a tower
made of solid ivory bone.

"Oh, save me," cried Rapawnzul,
"from this evil feline crime!
I need to find a noble dog
to speak to me in rhyme!"

But time did pass. No dog came near.
No terrier. No hound.
Rapawnzul soon despaired
her curse would ever be unbound.

One day a maverick Beagle
on his travels, happened by,
beneath the ivory tower
and he heard Rapawnzul's cry.

20

At first, he was quite speechless.
He could not rhyme a word.
For never in his dog-days
had so sweet a howl he heard.

And this was no mere mongrel,
no mangy mutt, no stray.
It was the boogie bugler
from the *Beagle Boys Brigade!*

They cut the hottest records.
Their songs were all the rage.
The Beagle boy declared at last,
". . . *She* should be on the stage!"

So with his paw across his heart
he swore to break the curse.
He fell upon his bended knee
and spoke to her in verse:

"I've climbed up Mount Olympus.
I've sailed the seven seas.
I've thrown myself upon the paws
of Princess Pekinese.

"I've chatted with Chihuahuas
in Tijuana Town.
I've herded sheep with sheepdogs
in Australia, upside down.

21

"I've lunched in France with Poodles
and eaten Crêpe Suzettes.
I dallied with some llamas
on a hillside in Tibet.

"I've played the boogie-woogie
with the *Beagle Boys Brigade*
and jammed with Fats Dalmation
on a famous Nashville stage.

"And yet your howl Rapawnzul,
is the best I've heard by far.
Your voice will make you famous—
and I'll make you a star!"

The Beagle's verse reversed the curse.
The ivory tower fell.
The boogie-woogie Beagle boy
had cured the Siamese spell.

Rapawnzul tucked her ears up,
and howling out in rhyme,
she chased the Siamese cat
around the castle one last time.

Then off went sweet Rapawnzul
to be famous with her friend.
And both the dogs were happy ever after . . .
that's

The End !

Finally! I was beginning to think we'd never get to be in one of these silly stories! How do I look?

Please! I need a moment of quiet to practice my lines.

Attention, please!

May we have your attention, please?

Just to show how gullible all dogs are, my noble companion and I would like to tell you the classic tale of...

THE DOBERMAN'S NEW CLOTHES

Once upon a time, long ago, there lived a great king named Doberman. King Doberman was handsome and sleek, and he had shiny black and tan fur, but he loved colorful clothing. Being of royal blood and having extravagant tastes, King Doberman wore all the finest clothes and fanciest collars. Soon, every canine in the kingdom followed suit and no dogs dared to be caught in public with just their fur on. King Doberman was so concerned with his appearance that he cared little for the common dogs of his kingdom.

23

He didn't care where their next bone came from, whether they had ticks or fleas or where they slept when it snowed. All he cared about were *his* new clothes.

One day, a pair of conniving cats came to town. "We are master tailors," the cats said. "We are able to cut the finest of cloth with our razor-sharp claws and to make the most splendid of canine clothes." They set up shop and hung out their shingle: *The Canine's Couturiers*. Well, that certainly got the King's attention. "Wow," barked the King. "Bow Wow! Let's see those clothes!" But that wasn't all the conniving cats told the King. No! The cats also told him that the clothes they made were magic—that they would be invisible to any dog in the kingdom who was too dog-gone dumb to see them. Now the King really wanted some of those clothes. "If I wore these clothes," thought King Doberman, "I would finally know who in my kingdom is truly clever.

All dogs are dog-gone dumb!

24

Only the cleverest of dogs would be able to see my clothes!" So it was settled. The King ordered himself a complete wardrobe.

A few days went by. Since King Doberman was not the most patient of dogs, he sent his trusted advisor and dogsbody Lord Labrador to see how the clothes were coming along. "If any dog is truly clever," said the King, "it is you, Lord Labrador. After myself, you are the smartest dog in the kingdom!" "Thank you," said Lord Labrador, and off he went to see the clothes. But woe! Woof! Whimper! When Lord Labrador arrived at the swindling cats' room he could not see the clothes. "Why, the poor pup's speechless," snickered the cats. "What's the matter, mutt? Cat got your tongue?" Lord Labrador looked and looked. He opened and shut his big, brown eyes. He shook his floppy ears till they flapped against his head—but it was no use. All he could see was an empty hanger held high in the air! "Am I barking up the wrong tree," he wondered secretly to himself. "Or am I dog-gone dumb?" "What do you think? Is that a fantastic fur coat, or what?" asked one of the conniving cats. Lord Labrador was dumbfounded.

Don't be ridiculous! Dogs don't think!

"It's . . . it's . . . unbelievable!" he howled and off he bounded back to the King.

Each day, King Doberman sent another trustworthy aide to see how the tailors were doing, but no one could see the King's new clothes. Not Baron Bulldog. Not Crown Prince Poodle. Not the Regal Beagle. Not even the Great Dane! And none of them would tell King Doberman that

they couldn't see the clothes. They were too afraid he would think they were dog-gone dumb! Instead, they said: "They're unimaginable!" "Out of sight!" cried Crown Prince Poodle. "I couldn't believe my eyes!" yowled the Regal Beagle. "Wow. Bow Wow," said the King. "I can't wait to see them for myself."

Eventually, the conniving cats sent word to the King that the clothes were ready. But when the King arrived to try them on, guess what? He couldn't see the clothes, either! Of course, *he* couldn't admit it. Hadn't his loyal subjects all seen the clothes? Hadn't they all described them as simply unbelievable? What could King Doberman do? He stripped down to his bare fur and pretended to put the clothes on. "They're so light!" he exclaimed. "It feels as though I'm not wearing anything at all. You truly are clever cats." And out the door he went.

The King set out to parade around the kingdom in his

new clothes. He held his head high and every dog in the kingdom stopped and stared as he walked by. "Wow," thought King Doberman. "Bow Wow! This suit must really be something. Look how everyone admires my new clothes!" The dogs gawked

But the King's not wearing any clothes!

and ogled and gasped in surprise, but no one was willing to admit that the King was, well—naked! No dog wanted to admit that he was dumb! Instead, every dog in the kingdom, even the mongrels and strays, ordered clothes from *The Canine's Couturiers.*

Each time they passed one another on the road, they would stop and sniff and admire each other's clothing. "Wow," they would say. "Bow Wow! Nice clothes!" Which explains how the conniving cats got so smug and why all dogs today run around without any clothes on!

the end

28

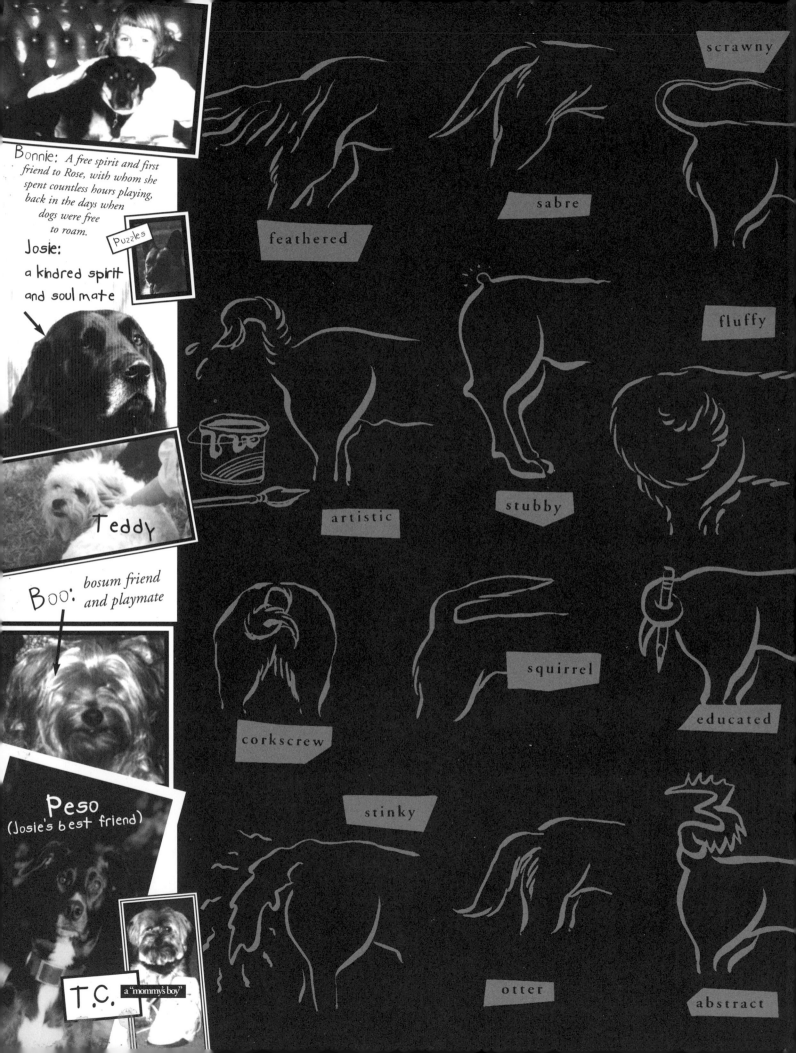

Bonnie: *A free spirit and first friend to Rose, with whom she spent countless hours playing, back in the days when dogs were free to roam.*

Puzzles

Josie: a kindred spirit and soul mate

Teddy

Boo: *bosum friend and playmate*

Peso (Josie's best friend)

T.C. a "mommy's boy"

scrawny

feathered

sabre

fluffy

artistic

stubby

corkscrew

squirrel

educated

stinky

otter

abstract